The Teddy Bears' Christmas

Pictures by
Prue Theobalds

Words adapted from the lyrics of
The Teddy Bears' Picnic
by Jimmy Kennedy

UPLANDS BOOKS

If you go down in the woods today
You're sure of a big surprise.

For Christopher

*The Illustrator would like to thank
the Jimmy Kennedy Estate for
allowing her to adapt the words
of The Teddy Bears' Picnic*

First published 1998 by
Uplands Books
1 The Uplands, Maze Hill, St Leonards, East Sussex TN38 0HL

This edition reprinted in 2002 exclusively for Advanced Marketing (UK) Ltd, Bicester, Oxfordshire.

*Reproduced by permission of
International Music Publications*

Illustrations © 1998 Prue Theobalds
The moral right of the author/illustrator has been asserted

If you go down in the woods today
You'd better go in disguise;

For ev'ry bear that ever there was
Will gather there for certain, because
Today's the day the Teddy Bears have
their Christmas.

Ev'ry Teddy Bear who's been good
Is sure of a treat today.

There's lots of marvellous
things to eat,

And wonderful games to play.

Beneath the trees
    where nobody sees
They'll hide and seek
    as long as they please,
'Cause that's the way
    the Teddy Bears have
    their Christmas.

If you go down in the woods today
You'd better not go alone.

It's lovely down in the woods today
But safer to stay at home.

Christmas time for Teddy Bears,

The little Teddy Bears are having a lovely time today.
Watch them, catch them unawares
And see them on their Christmas holiday.

See them gaily gad about,
They love to play and shout;
They never have any care;

At six o'clock their Mummies and Daddies
Will take them home to bed,
Because they're tired little Teddy Bears.